I0520853

Storylandia

The Wapshott Journal
of Fiction

Issue 13

The Wapshott Press

Storylandia, Issue 13, The Wapshott Journal of Fiction, ISSN 1947-5349, ISBN 978-0-9884093-3-0, is published at intervals by the Wapshott Press, PO Box 31513, Los Angeles, California, 90031-0513, telephone 323-201-7147. All correspondence can be sent The Wapshott Press, PO Box 31513, LA CA 90031-0513. Visit our website at www. WapshottPress.com This work is copyright © 2014 by Storylandia. The Wapshott Journal of Fiction, Los Angeles, California. "Three on the Bank" is copyright © 2013 Kelly Ann Jacobson and is reprinted here with the copyright owner's permission. Copyright for the cover artwork is held by the artist and is reprinted here with the copyright owner's permission.

Storylandia is always seeking quality original short stories, novelettes, and novellas. Please have a look at our submission guidelines at www.Storylandia.WapshottPress. com or email the editor at editor@wapshottpress.com

Many thanks to Kathleen Warner for the proofread and editorial support.

Cover: "Schofield Covered Bridge, Bucks County Pennsylvania," by Eric Allen Jacobson, www.americanphotostudio.com

Storylandia

The Wapshott Journal of Fiction

Founded in 2009

Issue 13, Summer 2014

Edited by Ginger Mayerson

Table of Contents

Three on the Bank   1
    Kelly Ann Jacobson

Kelly Ann Jacobson

Three on the Bank

Sam

When Sam was a young boy, he used to play in his grandparents' pool for hours. Because he was an only child, he had little to do but act out situations, and pretending to drown was his favorite. He would sink to the bottom of the large concrete rectangle, cross his legs Indian style, and push his arms upward to keep himself steady on the ground. As his breath began to run out he would look up at the white pinprick of sun in the distance, the rays making their way through the chlorinated liquid like refracted rainbows on oil patches, and wait until the very last second, when his whole body screamed for air and the panic forced him up up up towards the sky. Reborn, gasping for air, he floated like a baby on the surface of the lapping waves and let the sun warm his chilled skin.

The wedding party is the last to head to the reception, since the photographer insists on taking pictures on every level of the Italian gardens where Sam and Greta said their vows. She snaps shots every two seconds as

Sam gives his new wife a hand up the tall bus stairs, though Greta's face shows only her frustration at heaving her immense chiffon train everywhere, and Sam's face is already sore from his forced smiles. They are happy of course, but like all brides and grooms, they will be happier still when the stress of this day is over and they can relax with a bottle of champagne in their hotel suite and remind themselves why they went through a year of torturous planning in the first place.

The bus, at least a decade old, contains two stripper poles, one on their end; neon waves of pink and green lights over the windows; glass goblets hung on metal hooks over the bar; blue velvet seats with 80's style box prints polka-dotted over them; and smells of pine air freshener and age. The bus has made several trips back and forth between the reception hall / parking lot and the Italian gardens where Sam and Greta married, and after five trips, all of their guests have been safely ferried to the wine and cheese plates. The wedding party is the driver's last run before he can go home, already over an hour late, and Sam wonders whether seeing this side of a wedding every day makes the man love weddings or hate them.

Greta sits down first, taking up enough room for two people with her cake of a dress, and Sam sits down next to her after shoving some of the chiffon closer to her leg. He grazes her thigh with his hand, and she winks. She looks so beautiful in the strapless white gown, with her long brown hair down falling down both sides of her face and decorated by twigs of baby's breath, and though the dress cost five thousand dollars, it seems worth every penny. Her necklace is the one he gave her for their one year anniversary, a small chain with a tiny bunch of dangling diamonds on the end, which she has worn on all special occasions for the past five years.

"Down, boy," his best man Joe teases as he sits next to Sam. "You have to get through the party first." Sam punches Joe's arm, and in turn Joe shoulders Greta's brother Luis, who shoulders his wife Maria, who shoulders Greta's best friend.

"Behave, you two!" Sam's mother says from across the aisle, like she used to when they were little and did something stupid like dig up old Ms. Mendez's tulips. "You're married now," she looks at Joe, "well, one of you is, so you need to settle down. Let my future grandchildren do the misbehaving from now on."

Sam and Greta try not to look at each other when she says that, but almost immediately they catch each other's eye and blush. If only his mother knew what they do: there is already a grandchild on the way. Just a week before their wedding Greta called him from home, strange since she should have been teaching that day, and of course he answered even though he was already a few minutes late for an important deposition. That night he touched the warm flesh of her stomach and imagined the baby growing like a star inside of her, and she put her hand on his, and they lay like that for a long time until they fell asleep.

Once everyone is seated and comfortable—except Greta's friend Jen, who stands near the stripper pole and pretends to dance to catch Joe's eye—the bus takes off with a lurch and descends down the slope of mountain that leads to the reception hall. The driver asks the wedding party to entertain him with embarrassing stories about the bride and groom, and all of their friends jump on the chance to give their own speeches to embarrass the couple. Joe brings up the night Sam met Greta at one of their favorite bars in Philadelphia: he saw Greta at the other end of the bar and was too shy to go over and talk to her, so Joe went to talk to Greta's friend instead. Joe was wickedly rejected, but in the meantime, Sam struck up a conversation with Greta. While he gave what he thought was an impressive description of his job, he spilled beer all over his pants, the nearest stool, and the floor beneath it, then mopped the liquid up with what he thought was a napkin but was actually Greta's scarf.

"The saving grace," Joe says loudly to the rest of the bus, "was that he unknowingly brought up a case we did pro bono for a children's organization in Philadelphia that Greta happened to volunteer for. Suddenly WHAM: she couldn't take her eyes off him, beer stains and all. And because of that one moment, here we all are two years later, celebrating their marriage."

"Life is crazy," the bus driver says. "Your whole life can change in just one moment."

He must be in his late forties, though he looks about eighty with his long ginger beard and smoke-stained teeth. Even the required uniform cannot clean this man up, but he has a genuine smile and was patient with the older attendees when they took ten minutes to climb the stairs. Plus, Sam thinks, not much more can be expected from a rural Pennsylvanian.

The bus bumps over the start of a bridge, then hits a misplaced wooden plank and bumps again. Jen, who has been standing this whole time, falls into the lap of one of the groomsmen. The driver turns back to check on her and immediately starts apologizing, though the condition of the bridge is obviously not his fault; everyone looks towards Jen except Sam, who turns away so he won't see up her skirt when she tries to get up.

Because of his modesty, he is the only one watching the road when the bus slowly veers into the side of the bridge and hits the guard rail. Everyone is thrown sideways into the aisle or windows on impact, and the driver falls from his seat into the stairwell.

"Oh no," Greta whispers from next to Sam as the bus leans in slow motion and then begins to fall, and she grabs his hand as their friends and family fall around them like meteors, trailing lines of bright dresses and loud screams behind them. His mother is somewhere towards the front, he can hear her yell, and then they are all thrown again when the bus slaps the water with a loud crack.

When they hit, Sam's arm cushions his head. He can feel the bones in his right hand break, but better them than his skull. Some of the bridal party scream, and though for all he knows he could be one of them; Sam cannot hear anything but a high pitched buzz and the rush of adrenaline and blood inside his own head. His vision blurs, body already in survival mode, and subconsciously he avoids eye contact with the splatters of red everywhere.

Instead, Sam focuses instead on Greta. Their hands were separated in the fall, but he can see her a few feet over. There is already water coming through a broken window below them, and though she is wet from the river, he does not see her moving in reaction. Her dress is stained a light pink from the lapping water (he hopes, he prays, it is not from her), and he keeps his eyes on her dress as he crawls through the water to her. She is not breathing, he can hear nothing from her open mouth nor feel a pulse with the hand that is not broken. Too late, he sees a piece of glass sticking out like a jagged mountain peak.

He screams, but no one is conscious enough to echo him or respond, and he keeps screaming as the water gets higher and higher around him. Then, when he has decided he will let the water take him, he feels his body numb, and before he knows it, he is climbing up the cushions of the other side of the bus, breaking a window, and pushing himself out despite the glass edge tearing into his skin. The bus sinks down with a lurch, and as Sam throws himself from the side into the cold water in an automatic response to survive, he prays to God: *let me die.*

It is not until he reaches the bank, spits dirty water from his mouth, and sees that he is the sole survivor, that he finally passes into oblivion.

Sam wakes to the burning of his skin in the afternoon sunlight. He is on a bank of some sort—the ground is composed of small brown pebbles and sharp gray rocks, and there are green reeds near where he lies— and above him on the bridge he sees a few spectators pointing to him and yelling. Not wedding guests, but campers dressed in hiking gear and those ridiculous backpacks people use to carry far too much for an unnatural length of time. He can barely hear their voices through the water in his ears, but he knows the female camper is extremely upset by the perfect O of her mouth and the way she keeps jumping and pointing a finger in his direction.

The man next to her tries to quiet her down, but when that doesn't work, he grabs her in a bear hug. Once she seems to compose herself, the male camper leaves her to climb down Sam's side of the bank while she runs back the way they came.

Despite their mountain-dweller appearance, the man takes far too long to get down the steep slope. He keeps slipping on pebbles (he is not grounding his feet before he steps, Sam notices, and he has poor balance), and on the final leap he skids on one foot and almost breaks his ankle. Close-up he is much older than he looked from far away, almost fifty, with a red and white speckled beard and thin matching hair peeking out from under his hat. Sam has not moved during the stranger's journey, though he is aware that his arm is asleep and his hip is twisted at an unnatural angle.

"Holy shit dude," the guy says as he gets closer, and Sam wants to roll his eyes at the granola-crunching hippie slang but cannot move or feel any part of his body. Either everything is broken, or he is in shock. "I've never been so scared in my life. We saw the bus go over, and we ran, and the whole thing went down, and we figured everyone was done for, but then your head popped out of the water." When he gets close enough to see Sam's cuts and scrapes, he whistles. "You don't look good. Good thing my wife went to call an ambulance."

"Anyone else...?" Even his mouth is frozen, and the rest of his words build up behind his lips like a line of wrecked cars.

"Not that we've seen. I don't think we should move you unless absolutely necessary. The medics will know what to do when they get here." The man sits down next to him and begins to inspect him, and as he does so he tries to keep Sam talking. "What was it, a tour bus? Was anyone else with you?"

"Wedding bus."

The man hits a sore rib and Sam feels a jab of pain like a punch.

"Man... What was your relation?"

"Just a distant cousin of the bride." Sam does not hesitate as he lies—there will be time for pity later, when the medics come and ask for his ID and the truth comes out. For just a few minutes longer he wants to be anonymous, someone who will walk away from the crash shaken but ultimately unaltered. For just a few minutes, he cradles his normal life.

In the hospital, he says little to anyone unless asked a direct question. The nurses are careful around him and touch him like he is made of glass, and maybe he is. He has not cried, has not yelled, has barely reacted when the news stations showed search parties wading through the muddy water for remains. The hospital shrink, an apparent requirement during his stay, claims he is in shock, traumatized, but volatile—that the wrong word will set him off and he will explode.

"Are you angry?" the shrink asks him as he rubs what is left of his balding hair.

"No."

"Are you angry at yourself?"

"No."

"Are you angry at God?"

"No."

"Why not?"

"There is no God."

They keep all sharp objects away from him, keep him in the ward with a guard. The psychologist calls in a specialist from California, a middle-aged man with a large yellow notepad that he rests on his enormous stomach.

"You need to face your denial," the large man says as he looks at his watch. His lips are round and wet, like slick stones on the beach, and he licks them after every comment as though he is wetting a reed.

"I'm not in denial."

"That's what all people in denial say. It's the first sign." They both look at his watch.

"I watched my entire family drown in front of me. It's a little hard to deny what you see with your own eyes."

After two hours of notes about Sam's curt responses, the famous doctor gets little more out of Sam than his predecessor. "I leave him in your capable hands," the new doctor says to the old, eager to get back to the paying patients with body image issues and high levels of anxiety. "I've done all I can."

The medical doctor has more concrete conclusions to report: broken arm, mild concussion, bruises on both legs the size of a handprint, three large scrapes. For surviving a crash like that one—a twenty foot fall in a bus, an almost-drowning, a swim through the jagged glass of the window—the doctor tells him he is a lucky man. Lucky: Sam's new defining adjective, the one that started with the hiker and continues as the mantra of the newscasters who repeat it over and over again. He wants to tell them they should be so lucky, but instead he keeps quiet, stares at the wall, is careful to answer questions directed at him when necessary. They feed him green jello, almost-frozen sandwiches, cold soup... prisoners eat better than hospital patients, though he eats it all dutifully. In the hospital he is a caged dog, a freak show for reporters who try to sneak in for an interview, and he wants out.

Two weeks later they release him. They have no choice—without any life-threatening injuries his insurance is clamoring for his release. He emerges into the blinding, sunny world with blinking eyes and tingling skin, like a newborn but with all the knowledge of an old man. His car was towed to his house from the wedding venue, a hefty bill probably put on his credit card, so he calls a cab from outside the hospital wing and waits on one of the green metal benches for its arrival. He knows the next few steps already: sell the house, rent a room, and attend the rest of the funerals. These are things he must do, and the doctors and professionals will watch him closely for another month to make sure he does so without complication.

Luckily the families of the dead think of him as a loose cannon, someone not to be trifled with, so there is little he must do in terms of planning besides show his face. He stands like the headliner of a show, and other people move around him in anxious circles, standing at least two feet away even when they pass him in a hallway. They learn quickly that he does not want to hug; he does not want to reminisce about the distant memories they have with the lost members of his family; he does not want their pity or their attention. Occasionally someone tells him in his or her best sympathetic voice: "This must be so hard for you," and he thinks *not harder than watching them drown as I swam to safety* but remembers that they expect him to keep it together. All he wants is to be left alone, to be the last man standing in the corner when the food is gone and the guests are tired from the wine and cheese plates, to be sent home.

They never find his mother's body—an empty jar represents her remains—and when he picks up her ashes he thinks of how they used to play pranks on each other, like the time she set up a row of five sprinklers in the grass and set them off as Sam stepped outside into a bright new day. He avoids remembering the part where his father yelled at her for drenching the boy and thereafter the carpets, and the part where he called her a child.

Greta's funeral is last, and for a week beforehand he swallows the little blue pills that shift him into sleep by late afternoon. He must avoid the daydreams, the screams he never heard but can remember all the same, like howling wind through the branches of the trees outside of his window; he must make it to Sunday before he sinks beneath the waves.

When he arrives at the church the first thing he thinks is *Who's getting married?* Lilies line the aisle and spill from large vases on either side of the alter like a nervous bride and groom, and the ushers hand out pamphlets with the same pictures of Greta that were on their wedding website. In one she stands between her two best friends, both dead now, at a fundraiser for whatever nonprofit she worked for at the time. The three girls hold large glasses of sangria towards the picture-taker, a perpetual toast to the viewer, and all three are laughing. Sam recognizes her favorite ash-colored pantsuit, an outfit which caused many late mornings because he couldn't keep his hands off of her in the tight fitting gray pants, and her hair is straighter and longer than he remembers. When no one is looking he slips another pill into his mouth and swallows the smooth plastic-coated savior without water.

It is like a drinking game: every time someone says the name Greta, he falls a little deeper into the drug-induced high of the pills and the pot he smoked in the church parking lot. He thinks of this high as a wishing well, an imaginary safe place where *Greta, Greta, Greta* echoes down and the only other sounds are the drip of water and the occasional call from penny throwers. *Greta was kind, Greta was loved, Greta will be missed,* step step step, and the room spins around him until he must lie down against the wooden pew or risk passing out. A distant cousin of Greta's carries him to the car and drives him home, sparing him the sound of dirt shoveled against her wooden casket.

Their apartment, or what is left of it, is like a car after a metal-crunching wreck. Part of the mess is practical—Sam was in the hospital, so the dishes and trash festered for weeks while he did the same in his small cot—and after that he was too busy attending funerals and getting high to clean. But most of the rubble is from his nightly drunken quakes, the shaking of his world like a boat in the storm, and if he picks up anything he immediately drops it on the floor or throws it at a wall. The remains of the food he manages to scarf down are scattered evenly over the wasteland of the carpet and wood floor, though once in a while he shoves an empty take-out container or plastic bag towards the perimeter with his foot. The mail is in layers on the coffee table near the door, and whenever he shuts it violently, one or two envelopes slide off the others.

After he puts the containers of food the mothers, aunts, and female cousins of the deceased insisted he take home with him in the overflowing trash can, he throws his shoes off and removes his shirt, shedding it like extra skin. Then he falls onto what should have been he and Greta's marriage bed, coverless since the laundry has sat in the washer since the day before the accident, and stares at the ceiling until sleep takes him.

* * *

Marissa

Marissa leaves the bar exhausted, with enough money in her pocket to last through the expenses of the next three days: the phone bill, electric bill, Joey's field trip, plus a few extra bucks for a snack and a souvenir. The money weighs next to her thigh like a camel hump full of twenties and tens, bills paper-thin but heavy with the hundreds of ways they can be divided. Endless permutations, spinning like lottery wheels until they line up with the cheapest way to fulfill every responsibility. On good days, she can even buy her favorite cheese blintzes from the diner on the corner while the sitter helps Joey brush his teeth and kisses the elephant stuffed animal his father bought him years ago. Marissa can almost feel the thick chunks of cheese filling and flakes of fried pancake in her mouth, swirl the blueberry juice, swim in the pleasure of a meal she didn't make with company who is not her son or a grasping patron.

Outside the bar she finds the bus bench empty and unloads her heavy backpack onto the flaked wood, puts on her headphones, rests her head on the back of the bench, and breathes. The night is quiet; at 2:00 AM she feels like the only one in suburban Philadelphia awake, the only one staring at the stars waiting for the tired bus driver to screech her way past the stop and then halt just long enough for Marissa to jump on. Sometimes she waves the two dollar fee with a quick flick of the wrist, her own tired eyes recognizing the craterous darkness of a fellow night-dweller, and other times the driver is looking out the window as she stops, savoring her one moment of freedom before she plugs forth into the darkness.

Over half an hour to home: enough time for

Marissa to listen to a few songs, or read a couple pages of a book, or glance at the news so the world stops happening without her notice. Or just look at the passing houses as they get smaller and smaller, closer together, stacked on top of each other, and become the government-sponsored version of a slum. As they get closer to Marissa's house there are less street lights and less cops, as though they are giving a free pass to those who want to spread the chokehold on the single mothers and desperate fathers and young people just trying to make it. She works hard so that one day she will bring her boxes to the landing on apartment 2G, pack them in a moving truck, and carry Joey away from the frayed carpets and the smell of the neighbors' dog and the worry that comes with letting her son go to school every day.

Finally she pulls the wire and hears the accompanying bell that means she is almost there. Standing feels strange to her fatigued legs, and she has to hold the handrail to keep from sinking to the bus floor. After she exits with a quick wave at the driver, who nods back to her in the rear-view mirror, the bus speeds away to its final destination with a burst of exhaust and a whine of the wheels. The homeless man who wanders their neighborhood is missing from his nightly post at the bench, the hour too late for even his angry glare. She walks the street alone, not a car or pedestrian to break up the chilly autumn, and notices the sun is already sending rays over the edge of the world.

When she gets to their apartment she opens the door as slowly as possible and closes it gently behind her, careful not to wake Joey or the neighbors below. The place is as she left it—dishes on the dining room table, clothes strewn on the couch from when she changed before work, pots on the stove filled with congealed macaroni and cheese. After hours of closing clean-up at the bar, the last thing she wants to do is more work; instead, she shoves all of the stuff on the floor to the far corners of the living room, pulls the living room coffee table into the dining room, and changes back into the leggings and over-sized t-shirt she was wearing before work.

Marissa puts on music: the CD her former boyfriend, Paul, made her during their dating days, a mix of lyrical slow songs, fast jazz, and hip-hop. She fast forwards to number five, a love song—their song—Elton John's "Tiny Dancer." Paul used to call her that, and every time he would hoist her up and swing her around to prove how tiny she really was, she felt like a small child in her father's arms. If the baby was asleep she would wrap her legs around Paul and kiss him, and he would lift her closer and then use one arm to squeeze her tight against his chest.

She thinks back to the night when she left the dance recital with her friends, relieved to be out of her tights and leotard and back in jeans. Joey was waiting for someone by the door, and her first memory of him was his leg, propped up like a bird. Everything about him was so dark that he seemed to be an extension of the wall: skin like wet dirt, brown eyes the color of a crack in bark, black t-shirt without a logo. The only thing that stood out to her was that leg... that and the way he came towards her, propelling himself by shoving his foot off the wall. It was graceful, the way he arched his shoulders over an invisible barrier and landed; she would find out later that Paul was a man who was only comfortable off-kilter.

"Hey," he called out as he swooped back up into a quick walk towards her. She turned and for a second could not see him, but then he was away from the wall and more visible against the lights of the parking lot.

"Can I help you?" She eyed him and crossed her arms, and her friends stopped and stood just far enough away to let them talk but close enough to intervene if needed.

"I saw you dance in there. Your solo was great."

She looked for sarcasm in his expression, but he stared back the way a scientist eyes a new find under a microscope: not just interested but invested, with hunched shoulders and held breath.

"Thanks." She had not seen him around campus, so she asked: "What are you doing at a dance department recital? Do you go here?"

"No, not really."

"Not really?"

"I went here for a little bit, but I'm taking some time off now."

"Doing…?"

"Music. Guitar. And working in my dad's car shop."

"Are you here with someone?"

He looked down at his shoes, black leather scuffed at the toe and the sides but otherwise well cared for. "I came to watch a friend."

So he had a girlfriend; he was just being a nice audience-member. "Well, thanks, and it was nice to meet you. I'm Marissa by the way."

"Paul."

She gave him a small salute, then turned on her foot and dropped into a small lunge before starting to catch up with her friends.

"Wait," he said, grabbing her arm. She tried to pull her hand from his grasp, but instead of letting go, he threw her slightly forward and then twirled her back towards him. For a second his heat came through the wool jacket, and she warmed herself from it.

"The friend is my dance partner," he said by way of explanation. "Dana McDonald. She's my neighbor, and she asked me to join the salsa club at school back in the day." She knew the name, had seen the girl in a few of the Intermediate Ballet classes. She was no threat in the looks department: frizzy red hair, short pudgy legs, lack of grace in her movements. "If you wait a minute, we can all go out together."

Already he was leading her—though he did not touch her again she could imagine him putting out his hand and drawing her close, encircling her waist, pushing her hand up with his and looking her in the eyes. She told her friends to go on to the pizza joint and they would meet them there, all without taking her eyes off of Paul. When Dana showed up, Marissa barely noticed.

The next morning she wakes up sore, and the aches in her thighs and hamstrings yet again signal the decline of her previously fit dancer's body. She can still kick as high, can still turn as fast, but the recovery time is twice as long as it used to be. The alarm says 7:20 AM, already twenty minutes late, and though all she wants it to turn over and let herself sink into the loving arms of sleep, there are too many things she has to do. Joey leaves for school by 8:00 AM, so she must leave a one-hour oasis between her sleeps to get him up and ready.

The covers come off first, thrown with a whoosh of air like a parachute, and then both feet hit on the floor. Her head aches, though she has the shots the night before, not the dancing, to blame for that. For a second she pauses and puts her head in her hands until the room stops spinning, and then she propels her body into the air and gives it a quick shake.

"Mom, you up?" she hears from the bathroom, and she yells back that she's as up as she'll ever be. It amazes her that her little seven year old can set an alarm, wake up, and put himself in the shower all before mom is up to knock on his door; she still remembers the days when she threw pillows at her sister when she came to wake her up, or clung to the railing of her bed when her mom grabbed her legs and tried to pull her out. Then again, she had the luxury of assuming someone would always be there to force her out of her dreams.

When she gets to the kitchen, she stops at the entranceway and stares at the spread Joey has set up for them. In front of each of their spots are perfectly folded napkins on the left with spoons lounging on them, bowls filled with cereal (hers with a granola mix and his with one of his sugary snack-cereals, but not milk—they will pour that in when they sit down to eat together), little glass cups of orange juice already sweating. A sliced banana is on display on a plate in the middle, with forks next to it so they can share it by stretching and spearing a piece.

Marissa wants to cry, but if she lets herself cry at every grown-up act that boy does, she will never stop crying. Instead, she packs his lunch in his *Toy Story* tin box: peanut butter and jelly on soft wheat bread, sliced apple, a snack of peanuts and cashews and raisins she mixes in a large plastic tub they keep in the cabinet, 100% juice box. The healthy snacks are not forced on him; Joey is a naturally healthy eater, and he requests alternatives when they try to feed him candy or ice cream at school. By the age of four, he demanded to be taken to exercise classes so he could be "big and strong like Daddy." Dance she ruled out immediately, but consented to gymnastics and kickball club and soccer as alternatives.

"Mom, you okay?" she heard from behind her. She is staring into space again, still holding the small plastic container she will put the trail mix in. When she turns she sees him already dressed in a brown and black checkered flannel button-down and jeans, his curly brown hair brushed as well as it can be, black sneakers tied. His backpack is by the door, with all of his folders and papers zippered safely inside.

"Fine. When did you become such an adult?"

Joey looks pleased, and when he walks to his seat at the table, his shoulders are taller and pushed back. He aches to be an adult, to step into the shoes of his father; she can tell by the way he wants to do everything for himself and for her, when she lets him. She sees it in the way he makes lists of chores for the weekends, or keeps all of his play dates carefully listed on her calendar on the fridge.

"Last year." He grins at his own joke, and she ruffles his hair as they sit down. They pass the milk, of which Joey takes a good portion so he can eat his chocolate cereal out of it and then drink the chocolate milk, and then he crunches while she picks at hers. Her stomach twists at even the thought of eating, but he will worry about her if she doesn't.

"Mom, at school we're making three kinds of aquariums and terrariums: snails, crabs, and frogs. Then we all get to take turns bringing them home, but we can't take them on the bus. Can you come get me one day this week so I can bring one home?" 3:00 PM: to prepare for his noisy arrival at 4:00 she will still be in the cocoon of sleep so precious to her these days. Plus the fifteen minute drive each way, and the inability to go back to sleep Joey will want to explain every aspect of the terrarium.

"Sure, how about today?"

"You mean it?" His eyes are bright, and his small hand is slapped on the table like he is about to jump over it into her arms.

"I wouldn't say it if I didn't. I'll set my alarm a little early."

Joey gets out of his chair to take his bowl to the sink and does a little wiggle dance on the way. She can't help laughing, and to amuse him she gets up and does a jiggling dance too. He cracks up, and for the few precious minutes they have left together, both of them swivel their hips, make their knees give out to the sides, and wave their arms in the air.

The bus is already halfway down the block when he shoots from the door, backpack flailing from side to side on his small sweatered back, but she sees him get into line with the other neighborhood kids just in time. Their bus driver is Cindy, a frequent visitor at Frankie's Bar; Marissa once had a man thrown out because he was hassling the driver, so since then Cindy waits for Joey if he is a minute late.

The kitchen is a wreck, so she does the dishes from the past two days and wipes off the small wooden table just big enough for two—first she and Paul, then she and Joey, but never both. Then she brushes her teeth, takes off her bra, removes her socks, and falls back into bed, where dreams wait for her with a soft caress or sharp teeth.

Sam

Three months pass in what feels like ten years. Sam sleeps all day, so as not to be reminded of his wife by any of the activities they did together, and is awake all night watching mindless TV to match the static of his mind. He loses thirty pounds, his bones emerging like an archeological dig from the pale skin of his chest; he gets his first gray hairs at his temples, which he shaves off in a desperate attempt to stop time. The house becomes a tomb.

They turn his power off in a desperate attempt to freeze him out (the rent is on direct deposit, but Greta paid the smaller bills), but he plugs in his small electric heater, sits in a chair beside it to keep warm, and wears a thick skin of three dirty sweaters at all times until one of his relatives calls and straightens the matter out. The phone stays on for longer, but Sam rips the cord from the wall so the thousands of apologetic callers leave him alone. He has no interest in Greta's childhood friends, or their double-daters who want him to come out as a third wheel, or the relatives abroad who want to ease their guilt for not attending the funeral by throwing help his way. If anyone wants to talk to him, they know where to find him… though it's not like he opens the door when people come knocking.

The only times Sam leaves the house are to get "groceries" (bags of chips, frozen pizza, alcohol) and to go to the bar down the street, Ginger's Bar and Grill. They know him there—it is the bar where he got drunk the night before Greta's funeral—and they do not bother him, not even to ask for his drink order. Ginger just brings him beer after beer, sometimes a pitcher if she is busy serving other customers, and charges him once a week; in return for her silence, Sam tips her fifty percent.

One night after a good two hours on his favorite bar stool watching sports and spacing out, the man next to him reaches critical mass and starts to yell at the girl next to him. From the look of it the woman is his wife, though it could be another man's ring on her finger. They are both in their mid-forties, and the kind of suburban Philadelphians he tries to avoid—old jeans, bad teeth, hair that needs to be cut, heavy smokers, TV watchers—but then again there is no longer a defining line between him and them. And no matter their differences, when the man starts yelling, the sound of his voice echoes through Sam's brain like an old fashioned alarm that shakes him up and bangs him awake.

"I know you're seeing someone," the man says to his wife, who rolls her eyes and takes another swig of her beer. "Just admit you're whoring around and I'll let this whole thing go. But don't act like I'm an idiot."

"You *are* an idiot," she tells him. "When do I have time to see anyone else when I'm the one working all day and you're home? I don't even get a lunch break."

The man stands up, the legs of his stool dragging behind him, and grabs her arm in an intimidating motion. The red spreads from his fingers over the woman's skin, and finally she looks scared.

"Hey buddy," Sam says before he thinks, "Why don't you settle down. It's Friday night, and the people in here just want to have a peaceful drink and relax." It is the first time he says anything in months even resembling a normal conversation, and the other regulars turn, shocked, to witness what has caused this change.

The man releases his wife's arm and turns slowly towards Sam. He is a small guy, at least six inches shorter and ten years older, but his muscles are lean and his face is tough from sun damage and scrapes. Probably rides a motorcycle and has chin-up contests. If they fight he will kill Sam, though Sam no longer cares.

The woman tugs at the man's arm, and before Sam can step in, her husband shoves her off of him and lunges towards his newfound nemesis. Sam ducks, and the man swings high and tips off-balance. Then the younger man shoulders him with all his power, all his anger, and the older man goes flying into the edge of the bar. "I'm going to kill him!" the man screams, but before Sam can even laugh, he feels a large hand grab him by the shirt and pull him towards the door.

Without looking, Sam swivels on his heel and decks the large man holding him up. It is only after his fist connects that he realizes who he hit: Lenny, the bouncer, a man who is so large when he stands behind the patrons he blocks out the light. He is about a foot taller than Sam, bald, and bulging with muscles like small animals inside of his over-tanned skin. A snake tattoo adorns the base of his neck and winds its way up to his ear, and both arms have sleeve tattoos of graveyards. The rumor amongst Ginger's patrons is that every time Lenny kills a man, he adds one tombstone to his arm.

"Shit, Lenny, I'm sorry," Sam starts to say, but before he can finish, Lenny hoists him by the shirt at least a foot in the air and throws him several feet onto a table. The old wood snaps beneath even his light weight, and he falls to the ground and hits his head on the wet concrete of the bar floor. The lights blink off one by one, and then he is unconscious.

He goes back to drinking at home and watching his own TV, not by his own accord, but because Lenny banned him from the premises. Days pass and then weeks, and every month would have continued to pass the same way except that one night as Sam stumbles through the house he trips on a pile of mail and grabs the counter to keep from falling. Under his hand is a flyer for a half-price drink night at one of the local bars, Frankie's Irish Pub, and at the bottom he sees "Now Hiring." What is it with bar owners and their own names? Yet he keeps coming back to the flyer all night, and he realizes that maybe he can work again after all, as long as he can keep his sleep schedule. There is nothing familiar to him in a bar, no memories to fight or run from, since Greta would never have set foot in a place like Ginger's or Frankie's.

The Frankie who owns Frankie's Irish Pub is just as Sam expected him to be: heavy accent, ten years past his prime, peppery grey and black hair, beer gut, loud laugh. Even from across the desk in the back office, Sam can smell the alcohol that permeates Frankie's skin and clothes after the thirty years he has owned the run-down bar near Sam's house. The desk across from his seat on a metal fold-out chair holds a computer monitor and a few spare papers, all that comprises the business side of Frankie's venture, and since he claims to spend less than ten minutes a day on paperwork and strategizing, Sam guesses what 'business' there is consists of luck and a dependence on regular customers. Hopefully Frankie has not heard the story of last weekend at Ginger's…

Before they can get started on the interview, the big old-school black phone on the desk rings and Frankie answers it with a quick flick of the wrist to his ear. Then: "Goddamn it Pam, I can't have you working shifts here when you're pregnant if you're going to call out every day. Either take time off or show up, but not both." Frankie (and Sam, who can't help but overhear) listens to the string of curses coming from the earpiece, and then Frankie tells her to come in the next day and hangs up while before the woman can say anything else.

"Looks like I'm working bar duty today. That's what I get for being an old softy and letting eight month pregnant women work in my bar. We'll have to finish this interview out front." He leads Sam back to the dining area, a spacious bar with ten wooden tables and a long counter that wraps around three of the four walls. From what Sam knows of this place, they move the tables on Thursday, Friday, and Saturday nights and have dancing for the locals.

Frankie goes to the serving side of the bar and bends down to grab fresh bottles, then inspects him over the worn wooden bar and asks in a doubtful voice: "Tell me, kid... why should I hire you?"

"Well..." Sam starts, then trails off. He used to be good at this type of thing—interviews, depositions, speeches in court, leading firm meetings—but he has nothing left to say. His head pounds from the many drinks he had the night before in preparation for this morning, and his stomach flips whenever he even thinks about food. Sitting was better, but now that he is standing he is afraid his knees might give out since he can feel them shaking under his jeans.

"You're a mess. You look like the last place you should work is a fucking bar. Hey wait a minute... Sam it was, eh?" Frankie tosses Sam a wet rag and motions with his eyes to the bar, so Sam begins to slowly wipe the rough surface with the warm cloth. It feels good to put his back into something, and he realizes he has not cleaned anything in months. "Sam Hamilton? As in the Sam that got busted at the bar down the street for fighting with that bouncer they've got over there?"

It seems word travels even faster in the bar world. "Yeah, that was me."

"But you don't have a scratch on you!" Frankie flips up glasses from under the bar as he talks, but he does not take his eyes off Sam. "I've seen that fellow—a big guy, mean as a black widow spider he is, but big as a mountain—I wouldn't fight him for my life. How'd you get out breathing?"

"I was lucky," Sam admits. "He threw me in the air, I landed on one of the tables five feet away, and the fall knocked me clean out. Even Lenny wouldn't hit an unconscious man."

Sam turns around and starts wiping the tables and chair down, and Frankie puts out a cup of peanuts and tells Sam he can help himself. The *tink tink tink* of the ceramic bowl is like rain on a tin roof, and his stomach growls even though he would not dare eat anything for fear of throwing up on the bar floor.

"What made you do it?" Frankie asks. He is turned away from Sam now, dunking glasses in a chlorinated tub with a whoosh and then setting them aside to dry.

"Do what?"

"Start a fight with a giant when you're just a wee man." Frankie turns around and looks him in the eye for the first time, and Sam knows he must give an honest answer or give up hope of getting a job.

"Size doesn't matter when you've got nothing left to lose."

The two men maintain eye contact for a few minutes, and then Frankie reaches under the bar one more time, pulls out a ball of black fabric, and flings it at Sam. He catches it with a little bit of difficulty and unrolls it, and the words Frankie's Bar in big yellow letters appear on a medium men's t-shirt.

"I'll hire ye', though I might regret it, because only men with nothing make it in this profession. Be here tomorrow at 9:00 PM to start your training."

The interview is the first time in over a month that Sam has been out in broad daylight, and when he steps out of the bar, the light blinds him like it would a miner walking out of a cave. Across the street there is a gas station convenience store where Sam is a frequent customer, and before he heads home he stops in to pick up a few groceries. Hatfield is dead during the day, and though there are no cars coming from either direction, it takes Sam a minute to realize he can cross. The only other person on the road is an elderly man waiting for the bus to the city on the corner diagonal to Sam, and though the old man tips his hat, Sam does not make eye contact or return the formality. *Just another few minutes and I'll be home*, he tells himself, and thinks of the way entering his house feels like sinking into a river with stones in his pocket.

When he enters the convenience store, the little bell dings above his head and an older Indian woman hustles from behind a curtain to serve him. He is used to Anna, the younger woman who is there at nights, but perhaps this woman is her mother. He can see a resemblance in their long black hair, quizzical eyes, and down-turned mouths. In less than a minute he selects a glazed doughnut, whole grain pretzel twists, banana, ice cream sandwich, and a Cherry Coke that begins to sweat in his warm hand. The woman (Samar, according to her name tag) looks at his pile of snacks and raises an eyebrow, and as she rings him up she sighs before she puts each item in the plastic bag. He has never seen a woman with this many gold bangles on her wrists—they cover her almost to the elbow, and when she reaches up to type they slide like an abacus back and forth on her dark skin.

Why do you own a convenience store if you disapprove of selling junk food? he wonders, and she gives him a quick shrug that he imagines means: *This is my husband's store, and therefore I am not responsible.* Then she glares at him when she thinks he is not looking, to add: *But you are.* He pays with one of his last twenties, a crumpled bill which the woman irons out with her hand, then leaves before she can tell him any parting words of wisdom like Anna does whenever he stops in. *You need a haircut, Smiling never hurt anyone,* and *That's a lot of beer for one person, I hope you're having a party* are Anna's stock phrases, and if this is Anna's mother, she probably knows about him and his habits.

On the walk home, Sam sees a few yellow leaves drift across the sidewalk in front of his feet like chased children. He looks to his right and sees the church where Greta attended Sunday services after the move—a church he has not entered since her death, despite the prompting of many of the overly-friendly members who dropped off tuna casseroles and lasagnas he let decay in their glassware until the smell prompted him to throw the containers away. He was never one for hugs and questions and discussions over plates of store-bought cookies, though his wife loved the neighborly concern that covered the congregation like pollen from a blooming tree. She soaked it up, just like she knew all of the names and ages of the children on the block, knew who had marital strife and whose in-laws were visiting. The social side to his quieter nature, she always took him by the hand and led him through a crowd of strangers to whom she introduced him as "My wonderful future husband."

Only around her did he feel wonderful; only when he dragged her, laughing, to the bed and lay there with her after a long day at the office did he feel like he could get through the tough parts of life. Even on the days when a client sent a PowerPoint presentation of the mistakes the firm made or his boss sent another secretary crying from the room, Greta was always there like a hot shower on a cold morning, ready to rejuvenate him so he could do it all again. And then she wasn't.

He finds himself, on an impulse he is not consciously aware of, turning onto the church's stone walkway and entering the cemetery behind the church. His feet move without him, numb and yet determined, like soldiers marching forward once their general is shot from his horse. After two weeks of funerals he attended dutifully with the help of every drug his doctor would prescribe, he vowed never to step foot in a cemetery until he died—yet here he is, again entering the world of the dead.

The cemetery is small, only about twenty feet in all directions, and the gravestones are all dark and cracked from age. They lean like trees in the wind, and their lilting stance makes him turn his head to the side to read the names. For once there are none he recognizes, no lightening to the heart at that moment when he connects the two wires together: your name is on this stone, and I knew you, and you are dead. For once it is a resting place of strangers.

He thinks he is alone, but then he hears the wheezing cough from behind him and turns to see an old, tall gray man sitting on a stone bench. A small bouquet of red roses lies in his hands, not yet given to whichever relative or friend he came to see. His white eyes stick to Sam, moving with him when he steps into the light and then back, until they are distracted by a gust of wind that blows more leaves across the dry grass.

Sam pretends to look for a name, then heads in the other direction towards a small stone and inspects it as though it holds the key to some mystery he must solve. He does not want the old man to talk to him, or to know that Sam is just passing through—he hates those visitors, the lucky people who want tingles up their spine as they walk over graves, or the etchings of names that belong to the dead and the ones they left behind.

"Did you know her?" the man asks from behind, and Sam sees a long finger point to the gravestone in front of him. A woman named Elena, dead for years. Before Sam was born.

"No, I didn't," Sam says abruptly. Get out of the conversation, fast.

"I know you didn't. That's my wife's grave you're standing on. So what are you really doing here, son?"

"Just passing through."

Both men are quiet for a few minutes. Then the man says: "Did you lose someone?"

There is something in his voice, the way it catches on the word someone, that tells Sam to stay just a minute longer. In a way, it feels good to have someone to stand with, even a stranger.

"Yes, I did."

"Recent?"

"Just a few months ago."

The old man shuffles his feet in the grass and leaves, kicking up a piece of green glass from an abandoned bottle. He is wearing the sneakers all old men wear: tan with small holes to let the heat out of their feet. If Sam makes it to that age, he will never buy a pair.

"Everyone tells you it gets easier," the old man says. "But it doesn't."

"So what do you do?"

He shrugs. "You keep going. That's all you can do, when there are people who need you. Just keep going, and remind yourself that you can't do the same; you're all that is left for everyone else."

"And if there is no one else?"

"There must be someone. Family member... girlfriend... friend...?"

"No one."

The old man turns to look at him, scanning his face for a sign of exaggeration, but does not find one. Sam has searched his own face many times in the mirror, and he knows what he looks like now: cold, like the concrete sidewalk behind them. Emotionless. Maybe the drugs, or the lack of sleep, or the numbness that wipes the life from his face like frost melting from a window. Then the man's eyes widen ever so slightly.

"You're that man from the news. The one they found on the river."

"That's me." The wind begins to pick up, and the bag in his hand clicks as the hanging plastic hits the other side. The trees rustle louder, as though the clouds coming in overhead are rubbing them with their hands.

"The dead have a way of hanging on, son, like leaches to the blood under your skin, and they just keep digging in until you are less human than husk. You've got to find a way to shake them off."

Sam remembers Greta's hand on his knee, the gentle pressure of her fingers, the way she slipped so quickly from his grasp. "I don't want to shake them off."

"I know you don't. The trouble is you don't have a choice. If you don't shake them off, you die."

He leaves the old man sitting near his wife's grave, the wind now at his back causing the plastic bag in his hand to crackle. After what seems like days he gets back to his apartment, the only place where no one can reach him, and yet when he shuts his eyes, the only thing he can see is the old man.

Despite Sam's obvious lack of bartending experience, Frankie schedules him to train on a Friday night, the busiest night of the week. He can hear the crowd of thirsty patrons halfway down the street, and he debates going back home... but to what? To half-dried pizza and reruns of shows he never liked the first time they played on public television? So he soldiers on down the road, takes a deep breath in front of the bar, and enters.

"Sam!" Frankie calls from the bar as soon as he walks in, and Sam looks around as he walks to the back and sees a few old men huddled over drinks. They must be the 'regulars' Frankie talks about like they are childhood friends; the men who shut the bar down every night after hours of reminiscing about lost loves and the home country, who are often too drunk to make it home after a long night of drinking and hitting on the younger women who wander in unknowingly and end up on Frankie's couch. Sam wonders what Frankie's wife must think of these strangers when she walks downstairs in the morning, but then again, she is probably accustomed to their imposition on her Saturday morning breakfasts. Maybe she drags them to church on Sundays to account for their sins, which he can imagine the old Irish men doing wholeheartedly only to turn around and drink again the next night.

Frankie introduces Sam to Marissa, the head

bartender on duty. She looks a few years younger than him, maybe about twenty-five, and has long brown hair that she braids in what Greta taught him was a French braid. He used to love watching her in the vanity mirror, hands stretched all the way behind her head, eyes closed, feeling the braid with her fingers as it grew thicker and thicker down the back; then he would hold a small hand mirror behind her so she could see her work, and pull her braid like they were children, and watch the O of surprise on her mouth and then the impish smile before she chased him around the room.

Marissa's face is bare of make-up, and she wears only a silver key on a chain around her neck, yet she is still beautiful, in the farm girl kind of way. If I were a woman working in a bar like this, Sam thinks, I'd be careful not to dress up too much either. He has not been this close to a woman in months, and it feels strange as she shows him how to mix drinks and puts her hands on his, overlaps their arms as she reaches for cocktail ingredients, touches his back lightly when she passes behind him.

Frankie heads home at 2:00 AM, leaving the closing duties to Marissa and Sam. "Train him well," he says to his head bartender, and she gives him a fake salute. "He'll be closing' up on his own soon enough."

As soon as the door closes, Marissa grabs two shot glasses and pours, then hands one to Sam. "Closing goes a lot faster with a little liquid fire in your blood," she tells him, downing the shot in one fast gulp. He watches her thin neck swallow, and then her eyes close as the alcohol hits her stomach. He has a strange urge to run a finger over her pale skin, wipe the drop of water from her mouth—amazing how the body works, how it desires even when the mind is numb – and then the image of Greta comes like a photo negative and all thoughts of touching anyone else disappear. If only she had not been perfect, had not been the most beautiful, kind woman he ever met... if only she had been average.

After a second shot Marissa yanks the scrunchie from her braid and unfolds the layers of hair until they fall loosely on her shoulders, then unties her apron. She tosses him a rag (what is it with bar workers and throwing things at each other?) and tells him to wipe the counters, tables, and appliances, then mop the floor and set the tables for the next morning. She says all of this in a detached yet demanding voice, never looking up from her own side work to check that he is listening. For such a thin woman she is extremely strong, and Sam doubts that if he tries to lift the tables or change the kegs he would not get past the first foot without giving up. He notices her hoist one of the buckets of water onto her hip, the natural curve of her back and side hugging the plastic tub like a child, and wonders if it is a practiced grip. Marissa is too young and small to be a mother, but then again, she's also too young to work sixty hours a week in a bar.

"You have a kid?" he asks, eyes on his cleaning but heart racing.

Marissa stops moving. "How did you know?"

"The way you were holding the keg earlier... it reminded me of how my sister-in-law used to hold her son."

She looks down for a minute, then her eyes lock with his. "It's a good guess. Yes, I do have a son; he's seven."

"What's his name?"

"Joey."

Sam hears the name and immediately his

esophagus constricts. He gags and then struggles to breathe, so Marissa runs around the bar and hits him on the back, hard. "I'm fine," he gets out mid-heave, but then his insides fight him and he runs to the bathroom and barely makes it. The chicken quesadilla he ate for dinner battles its way out of him, and then, empty of food, he continues to gag as he sits on the stained tile floor and puts his head against the cold wall behind him.

The smell of spilled beer and sweaty men after a night of drinking and dancing does nothing to cleanse his senses, and though he wants to leave the small prison of the restroom, he does not know how he can get out of the bar without Marissa stopping him to ask questions. He picks one thing to focus on: a scrawled name, Rose, with a small heart next to it. Not a round heart, the way small girls draw them on their notebook, but a tiny uneven red thing drawn by some drunk man one day when he was sitting there on the brink of passing out. Sam's eyes stay on the heart and memorize its lines; slip and slide on the upward arcs; get trapped in the V of the bottom half, until he can sit up straight without needing to vomit. Then he moves slowly, hand on the handicap railing, and straightens up.

Back in the bar, Marissa waits with a hand on her hip and a worried expression on her face. "Are you okay...?" she asks, and he recognizes her tone of voice as the same one his mother used to have when she knew he was about to lie and was warning him not to bother. He goes back to cleaning instead of answering, but Marissa watches him and stays in the same position until she forces him to look up at her.

"I know who you are," she says. "Frankie recognized your story from Ginger's, but it's not the only place he knows you from, is it?"

"I don't know what you mean."

"He knows you from the news, he just doesn't remember. We used to see that story on every day for a week: Sam Hamilton, the man who... well, I don't need to tell you."

No point in lying now, so he confesses it is him and waits for the questions. They are always the same: How did it happen? What did it feel like afterwards? How did you walk away unharmed? How do you go on every day? Or even worse, when someone tells him 'I couldn't do it if I were you,' as if surviving a tragedy is something he was bred for.

Instead Marissa drops her hand and starts counting the register. She starts with the bills and keeps track of the math on a slip of register tape, moving so fast that in the dim light the paper is a blur. Then she moves on to the change, and as she counts the quarters she begins to talk, but not about the accident or how he feels or what he will do now that everyone he cares about is dead.

"You didn't ask about Joey's father, like most people do. You didn't even look for a ring when you thought I was busy serving drinks."

"It's not my business." Sam grabs the broom and sweeps, but he watches Marissa from the corner of his eye.

"Damn straight. That's why I'll tell you someday... not today, but one day soon. Because you don't think you're entitled to it."

Marissa

The days and nights pass like shuffled cards. Sam improves at the bar; he drops fewer glasses, mixes more drinks, and gains confidence when talking to patrons. Occasionally he smiles. Neither of them bring up what happened on Sam's first day, and it seems like her co-worker prefers the distraction of the moment to digging up the past. They trade days off so Marissa can be home a few nights during the week with Joey to help him study for spelling tests or care for the soda bottle terrarium filled with snails he adopted (she couldn't resist his earnest face or how worried he got when one of them died, even though she had never been a fan of the sticky, gelatinous creatures).

Then one afternoon she checks her phone and finds three missed calls from Frankie. When she calls back he answers on the first ring, and he says her name before she can introduce herself.

"Have you heard from Sam?" he asks in a voice that is half angry, half worried.

"No, I haven't seen or talked to him since last Saturday night. Why?"

"He hasn't shown up for work in two days, and I'm starting to panic. Plus, I'm too old for all of these late nights. I've left him at least ten messages that would shock my mother if she heard them, god rest her soul, and still nothing. He's either sick or dead, and if it's not the second then when he shows up I'm going to kill him myself."

She thinks for a minute. She has a few hours left before Joey gets back from school; she could get on the 11:05 AM bus and be in Sam's neighborhood by 11:30 AM, check on him, and catch a cab back or get a ride from one of her friends. She grabs a pen. "Give me his apartment number. I'll find out what's going on."

At 11:27, Marissa gets one of the other residents to let her inside Sam's building and finds the number

Frankie gave her: 401. She knocks, softly at first and then louder and louder like an alarm, but still nothing. The woman who lives across the hall, a middle-aged woman in pink striped pajamas faded from many comfortable sleeps, eventually comes out instead. The sound of a cartoon show plays in the background behind her, along with an argument between two small children.

"You looking for Sam?" the woman asks, and Marissa confirms that she is and asks if the woman knows him. "Bit of a strange bird, that one. Do you know the story...?" The neighbor is eager to gossip and leans towards her, but Marissa is running out of time and cuts her off.

"Yes, he's my coworker. Do you know if he's home?"

Instead of answering, the woman looks at her sideways and then glances behind her to make sure the children are out of earshot and then brings her voice down to a whisper. "I knew them both, Sam and Greta, and it's not like how they say in the papers and on TV. I mean, yes they were in love, but they weren't perfect. The night before their wedding, I heard them shouting next door." She adds, "I wasn't eavesdropping or anything; these walls are paper-thin, and a person can't help but listen when the voices carry all the way to her bedroom."

Marissa knows she should not encourage this gossip, yet she finds herself asking, "What were they fighting about?"

"The bachelor party, from the sound of it. You know men—friends take them out, get them drunk, push them towards women in no clothes with large breasts and no responsibilities. Then they try to keep it all quiet, but we always know. So he comes home the next day at 3:00 AM, drunk and stumbling like all hell up and down the hallway, and she finds him an hour later asleep against the door with some other woman's lipstick smeared all over his face and down his chest. And she with a baby on the way."

Marissa is surprised—she did not know about the baby—but she tries to freeze her face so the woman will not see the revelation. There is already enough fuel to keep this bored housewife's fire burning for years to come, and poor Sam has been through enough without having a busybody prying into his affairs.

"Anyway, the night before the wedding they were arguing for hours, but by the morning it all seemed to be resolved. And then the bus went over the bridge, and it was all over."

It turns out the woman across the hall is the wife of the building owner, Mrs. Ray, so once Marissa tells her what she think happened to Sam, Mrs. Ray runs downstairs to find the ring of keys in her husband's office. She finally finds "401," puts the key in the lock, and turns. "I used to be a nurse," Mrs. Ray says, and Marissa tries not to think of what she expects to find that would necessitate those skills.

The inside of Sam's apartment looks like someone shook it like a snow globe. There is a pizza box on top of the TV, six pairs of shoes on the coffee table, baking pans on the chairs, and boxes and boxes of stuff stacked along the walls. Each one has just a name: "Greta," "Mom," "Greta," "Joey," "Greta." A few say "Sam," and are unopened. There is one box in the middle, the smallest box of all, that says "B."

He is not in the living room or kitchen, and by the time they get to the bedroom sweat is dripping down her back and her hands are shaking. She is afraid of what they will find when they swing the door open, but there is nowhere else to look. There are tracks of mud down the hallway, and the older woman whistles softly and says she hopes her husband doesn't see this anytime soon.

"You first," Mrs. Ray says, then points to the bedroom door. She is sweating too, and the sheen on her face matches the oil of her unwashed hair.

Marissa touches the doorknob, and for a second she feels the cool metal in her hand and prays: *please don't be dead, please don't be dead, please don't be dead.* Then she pushes, and the door swings open to reveal an entirely empty room, bare except for the single bed in the center and stripped of everything but the naked man lying in the middle of it. Marissa looks away immediately, and Mrs. Ray stares.

There is a bottle on the floor, and Mrs. Ray picks it up and reads it. "Sleeping pills," she says. Then she checks a few things, including his breathing, heart rate, and eyes under their heavy lids. "Just sleeping soundly," she decides. "Most of it is still in the bottle. Not enough to kill him. But if you take him in the hospital they might try to keep him there, a man with his history... But we can't leave him here."

"No. I'll take him home."

Mrs. Ray and Marissa dress Sam, who is semi-awake enough to mumble a few words neither of them can understand, then carry him down to a cab. "Take good care of him," Mrs. Ray says, and then she hugs her. "He needs someone."

By the time they get back to her house Sam is able to shuffle his way up the steps, after which she dumps him on the couch and he falls back to sleep.

"Is he dead?" Joey asks when he gets home, examining the new stranger under the blanket.

"No. Just sleeping, like you do on Saturdays

after a long school week."

Marissa calls Frankie, but she can tell by the heavy breathing on the other end that her boss's patience has run out. "I found him at home, and he's sick. I'll cover for him, and he'll be back tomorrow." Someone yells in the background, and then she heard the crash of broken glass.

"Get your butt in here in the next thirty minutes and you can both keep your jobs," he tells her, then hangs up.

Leaving her son with Sam worries her, but she has no choice. She calls Becky from across the hall and asks her to keep an eye on her apartment, then hands Joey her cell phone and goes over how to call the bar and Becky in case of emergency.

"Mom, I know how to use a cell phone..." he tells her with a roll of his eyes.

"Well I'm old and clueless, so I assume everyone else is too." Joey giggles, and she grabs him in a bear hug. "You're in charge," she tells him as she goes out the door. "If anything goes funny, call me right away. And Joey..."

"Yeah, Mom?"

"If he wakes up, take care of him. He needs it."

Sam

Sam wakes to the cackle and fry of cooking in the kitchen. Without opening his eyes he lets the soft vapors waft into his nose, and tries to guess: eggs, bacon, pancakes? Where is he, that such delicious smells envelope him in the first minutes of the morning?

When he finally pries his eyes open to a splitting headache, it is dim outside but the street lights are still on. The room is not familiar, but it has a familiar feel: the homey comfort of a living room with worn couches and empty cups on wooden coasters, like the one he grew up in. His clothes are the same as they were when he passed out in his apartment, but the shoes next to him on the floor are different; he has not worn his brown leather loafers since his days at the office.

His back cracks when he straightens, and the thick down comforter he does not recognize falls off his lap onto the floor. He throws one foot over the edge, then the other, and waits for feeling to return. Even wiggling his toes is a challenge, but eventually the blood winds its way through his veins into the extremities and he can stand after two tries. He makes his way, shaky at first and then more confident, towards the beckoning of the food smells from the kitchen.

When he arrives at the entranceway he blinks twice and then again to clear his vision. He must be hallucinating, because what he sees is impossible: there, in front of the stove, is a small child standing on a kitchen chair with a spatula in his hand. He is turned away from him, so all Sam can see is the maroon sweater and little pants, the straight brown hair slanted slightly to the right, the small fingers wrapped rightly around the much larger metal spatula. Then he trips over the trim between the linoleum kitchen floor and the carpet from the living room, and the small boy turns and smiles at him, then waves the spatula towards the kitchen table.

"Take a seat, Sam," the boy tells him.

"How do you know me?" Sam asks, but the boy gets distracted with whatever he is cooking and turns back away from him.

"I hope you like pancakes, because they're mom's favorite and she had a rough night last night. I'm making them as a surprise. Plus, she told me I was in charge of you."

"You're in charge of *me*? What are you, five?"

"Seven." The boy flips the pancakes on the big griddle in front of him. "And by the way, to answer your last question, my name is Joey."

Sam can't help wincing when he hears the name.

"Oh right, mom told me about that. Sorry about your family."

"Thanks." Sam rubs his forehead. He has a wicked hangover, and the pain is already in the center between his eyes and working its way across the skin to his temples. Dehydrated, he licks his lips but doesn't ask for water. He must be at Marissa's house, but he has no recollection of getting there or how long he has been asleep.

"Are they in heaven?" the boy asks, though he does not turn to make eye contact.

"Heaven?" Sam answers, secretly wondering how he can leave quickly without offending Marissa and her strange child.

"Yeah. Mom won't talk to me about it, but I've heard things at school."

"Oh. Maybe you should wait for her to talk to you about it." Sam pauses, then asks since they're on the subject: "Is that where your father is?"

"No. He's in New York–" Joey stops talking, closes his mouth and tilts his head to the side as he listens. "She's awake. Quick, set the table."

Sam has no choice but to listen, so he walks to the cabinet and takes out three white, chipped plates and three glasses and divvies them out, then goes back to rummage through the drawers for forks and knives.

"Left drawer, at the end," Joey directs without looking up, and Sam finds the drawer of a combination of at least five different sets of silverware. "Use the ones with the roses on the ends, those are her favorite."

"Whose favorite?" Sam hears from behind him, and he turns with the silverware in his hand like a thief caught in the act. Marissa stands three feet from him, dressed in sweatpants and a loose man's undershirt. When Greta woke she looked ready for a dinner party, tight black nightgown highlighting her curves, a little lip gloss she kept in the night stand next to the bed. Marissa is not a woman who worries about looking good for anyone—yet she does, with her long brown hair slightly messy and her black bra showing through the thin white fabric.

"Good morning, mom," Joey says, and she goes over to him and kisses him on the head.

"Good morning Joey-bear." Then she turns to Sam and says, "I wasn't sure if you'd still be here. How do you feel?"

"A little out of it... not tired, exactly, but sick. How did I...?"

She looks at Joey, then mouths the word *later*. She says, "You've been asleep for almost a day, I think." That explains the rumbling in his stomach, and the dizzy spells. "Today is Saturday."

Joey takes the pancakes off the griddle with a flourish of his wrist—enough pancakes to feed a family of six—then turns the griddle off and unplugs it just in case. He is so short that to get off the chair he sits down on it first, then scoots off and stands up to grab the plate with both arms. When he comes near the smell of fruity children's shampoo mixed with blueberry pancakes makes Sam's stomach rumble, and Joey gives him half of the stack of pancakes in response to the noise. Then he circles the small kitchen table to serve his mother two pancakes for which she trades him a kiss on the forehead, finally settles in his chair, and puts one perfect pancake on his own plate.

"Please pass the syrup," Joey says politely, but Sam does not hear him so he asks again. "May I please have some syrup, Sam?" When the syrup comes back around the table Sam discovers they have the good stuff, organic maple syrup the color of iced tea that absorbs into the pancakes before it has a chance to run off—a strange luxury in such a minimalistic apartment. He is careful not to let extra pour from the open spout.

"Oh, the coffee!" Joey exclaims before he can take a bite, and when he jumps up the chair scrapes against the linoleum. The sound echoes through Sam like an avalanche, and immediately his head goes back to its previous state of rebellion.

"Relax Joey, you've done enough," Marissa tells him, grabbing him by the shoulders and steering him back to his seat. She pours the coffee into two large mugs, both black, and puts one in front of Sam along with a small pitcher of cream and the sugar bowl. When he peers into the abyss of the mug it looks like a dark tunnel, endless, the kind he will fall into and never return from... he drops cream into the swirling liquid quickly, and the image disappears.

Marissa goes back and pours a tiny bit of coffee into a smaller black tea cup and gives it to Joey, who fills the cup with twice as much cream as coffee and a teaspoon of sugar. She shrugs towards Sam's inquisitive gaze without looking at him and says, "We drink it for the caffeine, but Joey actually likes the stuff."

"I love it!" Joey responds, slurping the cream-cooled coffee down and then putting the empty tea cup down carefully on the table. "What a perfect start to the morning."

"You're crazy," Marissa says in a voice filled with admiration, and Joey grins back at her. Then she remembers Sam, who has been silent most of the time, and the smile drops a little.

"You're supposed to work the lunch shift," she tells him matter-of-factly. "But if you go in looking like... well..."

"Shit?" Joey supplies.

"Joey!"

"Sorry..."

She sighs and then playfully swats his arm. "If you go in like that, they will take one look at you and send you back out the door. They can't have bartenders who show patrons how close they are to alcoholism."

"What's alcoholism?" Joey asks, and Marissa starts to rub her temple with her hand.

"What should I do?" Sam asks to change the subject, and she looks up and evaluates him.

The staring goes on a minute too long for anyone at the table, and then she says: "We can switch places. You can stay here with Joey, and I'll cover your shift for you."

Sam almost overturns the coffee he is in the middle of reaching for. He has never been responsible for a child of any age, let alone during the worst hangover of his life, and today does not seem like the time to try out his parenting skills. He starts to think of Greta but stops himself, and instead he says:

"You can't be serious."

"Why not?"

He has to remind himself to watch his tongue with Joey in the room. "You're going to trust me with your five year old son?"

"Seven," Joey pipes in.

"Whatever age he is he's a kid, and I don't do the kid thing."

"For your information," Joey begins, and his voice reaches the pitch of a learned professor, "I can take care of myself just fine. What she really wants it for me to watch over *you*."

"Ah. The kid has a point." He looks at Marissa, but she has gone back to rubbing her temples. Finally he addresses Joey directly: "Well, my fine guardian, I would love to hear your plan for caring for an old man on the brink of self-destruction."

Joey rolls his eyes, then counters with: "I think you're being dramatic," instead of asking what self-destruction means. It seems like something Marissa has told him in the past, and when he speaks he sounds just like her with that same blunt tone of voice and unforgiving edge. Then he says: "We can go to Oak Park."

A large open space filled with hundreds of children playing... Sam shudders , and though Joey misses it, Marissa looks at him and frowns. He cannot possibly bear it—even seeing a small child in the supermarket sends him to another aisle. How can he surround himself with giggles and bright pink jumpers, stuffed animals pitched across the jungle gym to a friend on the other side, sliding children assailing him from the dark green tunnels?

"That's a great idea," Marissa says, though she still watches Sam.

"I don't think-" he tries, but Joey runs to his bedroom to change before Sam can complete the sentence. He appeals to Marissa instead: "Why don't you take him, and I'll take the shift."

"You haven't seen yourself yet. Trust me, I don't love the idea of leaving my kid with a man who almost drank himself to death two days ago either, but if you walk in the bar they will fire you. Do you want to get the sack, or do you want to make an eager kid happy by taking him to the park?"

She does not wait for an answer—Marissa is not the type to ask a question she doesn't already know the answer to. Instead she gets up and starts the dishes, and Sam goes to the bathroom to see how bad the damage is.

"Wait," Marissa says from behind him, and he stops by the bathroom door while she hurries past him into her bedroom. She comes back with an extra t-shirt, black with a band name on it, and thrusts it into his hands. He opens it and sees it is a man's shirt, a little small but it will fit.

"Thanks," he says, but she is already gone. He closes the bathroom door and looks around. It is small but quaint, painted light blue with three sea shells in a wicker basket on the toilet tank. There is a faint smell of vanilla wafting from the air freshener plugged into the wall, the same fruity smell of Joey's shampoo, and he can tell no man has stepped in this house in a long time.

What he sees in the mirror makes him turn away in disgust. His eyes are bloodshot and as red as a burn mark, with dark half-moons underneath; his hair is disheveled and knotted; there are scratches on his neck that he does not remember getting and a bruise on his right arm. Has he been in another fight? Or was it a fall after clutching for a ledge to hold on to, broken bottle shards scattered on the floor, his blood wet like spilled milk on his arm?

The water he pools in his hands is cold and soothes his ragged face, and then he runs some through his hair and down his neck. A little bit goes down his temples into his eye, and he reaches for a towel blindly and feels his hand meet terrycloth. When he can open his eyes without stinging he sees it is a yellow towel with a little terrycloth cap made of the folded corner; the face of a duck stares at him from the outside, composed of a round red mouth and a big yellow beak. *A duck...*

"A duck!" Greta said, and she held the tiny rubber duck in the palm of her hand and then squeezed it to her chest. "It's perfect." The small plastic toy was part of a larger set of bath items he purchased that morning from a baby boutique down the street: a baby tub in the shape of a duck, two small towels with dancing ducks printed on them, three rubber duck toys, and a tiny shower cap with the words "I'm just ducky" printed in yellow letters across the top.

They had never thought about the baby's bath needs, but in the car on the way home one day Greta turned to him with guilt written all over her face and exclaimed: "Oh Sam, we've forgotten the bathtub!" Of course he had no idea what she was talking about, and at his confusion she began to tear up. "How are we going to be parents? We can't even remember that our baby needs to take a bath!" The baby was only a two month old fetus at the time, and they'd only known about it for two weeks.

Sam brings the yellow towel to his lips and feels the terrycloth like down against his skin. "I miss you," he whispers into the fabric. He speaks to Greta, but also to the little baby inside of her wherever she is now, and the words seem loud in the quiet bathroom. His fingers grip the material and turn white but still he cannot let go, so he sits like that until Joey calls him from the hallway.

Joey

Something is wrong with my mom's friend Sam. He looks the way I looked the time I got the flu and missed five days of school: small, defeated, blank like paper. When he goes into the bathroom after breakfast I can feel the darkness seeping under the door, and wherever he disappears to when he's alone is not somewhere I want to be. It reminds me of Mom when she thinks I'm not looking: her face sinks into a frown, her eyes glaze, and all of her muscles relax. When she looks like that she is visiting dad in her head.

I insist on going to the park after Mom leaves for work, and when she agrees to let Sam take me I know he is deep down in whatever he's in and she wants me to get him out. Like the time I found her crying in the bathtub, bubbles around her like ice caps in Antarctica, tears burrowing down through the layers into the hot water beneath. I took her hand, the one resting on my side of the tub not the one holding the wine stem, and I talked to her about my friend Lars and how he stuck a pencil up his nose the week before and the eraser got stuck. She laughed, and then she asked me to hand her the towel so she could get out. Her skin was pruny and red, and her hair was dry from sitting in the tub for so long except for the ends which looked like they were dipped in black paint. I covered my eyes with my hands until she said I could look, and when I opened my eyes she pulled me in to a bear hug and my clothes got damp.

After Mom leaves I pack us a snack while Sam watches: celery sticks with peanut butter and raisins on top, two juice boxes, two bags of sixteen crackers which is the recommended serving size for adults, and a banana to split since I don't like them very much. I put on my blue wool sweater and two undershirts so I won't catch a cold, and then I take a yellow sweater from my dad's drawer and give it to Sam to wear. It doesn't bother me much to see him in it since I never saw my dad wearing it, but I tell Sam to take it off before Mom gets home.

The park is only four blocks from the house, but Sam is a slow walker and he keeps turning to look at the old buildings and abandoned apartments on the side roads.

"It's not as bad as it looks," I say, even though it is. He doesn't say anything, so I keep talking: "I mostly worry about Mom walking around at night. I once read an article about a bus driver getting stabbed by someone on the bus and after that it was harder for me to sleep at night."

"I'd be worried too," he says, which is not what adults are supposed to say to kids when they are worried about something.

We get to the park and there are a few kids playing on the swings and littler ones in the sand lot next to the big slide, but none of them are my friends from school so I sit with Sam on one of the tables and explain to him about the park since he has never heard of it:

"The park was a community project, and people who helped build it have a wooden slat in the fence with their names on it. They made musical instruments in that room over there," I point, "and two separate ways to get up the top viewing tower and big blue slide. It's supposed to look like a castle, and there used to be a blue flag with a picture of a castle on it before one of the older kids stole it." It smells like damp wood and suntan lotion, which is probably coming from us since I put it on this morning.

"Pretty impressive." He doesn't look impressed.

"Want to go up with me?" I ask, and Sam looks skeptically up through the wooden slats to the top of the castle where the big slide's entrance is.

"Don't you think I'm a little big for a slide?"

"Nope. They made it for kids and adults. Mom goes up with me all the time."

He sighs, and though he obviously does not want to climb up I insist. For some reason I feel like if he goes up into the castle something magical will happen, like in *The Sword in the Stone* which is my favorite movie, and that as he climbs whatever he worries about will fall away onto the steps like water from wet hair will bounce all the way down the thirty-five steps and the kids coming up will walk on the worries and squish them under their feet.

We go all the way up, and Sam has to duck so he won't hit his head on the low beams. We climb over the rope floor on the middle level of the castle, and I stop to look down at the kids two floors below us through the squares of blank space between ropes. Sam holds on to the wood on both sides of us, and I can tell he is scared by the way he grips the slats too tightly and hesitates before lifting each foot.

"It's safe," I tell him, doing a little dance across the rest of the ropes.

"I don't do bridges," he says, still walking slowly towards me as I wait on the other side.

"This isn't a bridge. It's a rope floor."

"I guess that's one way to look at it." He finally gets across, and I make a mental note to take him up the other way if he wants to ride the slide a second time. Then I lead him to the highest watch tower, the room with the slide, and because it's still early and not many people are here yet we get the whole room to ourselves.

"What was it like?" I ask because I have been wondering the whole day but holding myself back from asking.

He doesn't ask what I mean. Instead he looks out over the park, and we listen to the happy screams of children going higher and higher on the swings. I want to apologize for asking, but I don't know how.

"Have you ever seen video of an earthquake?" he asks.

"Yes, on the news once."

"It was like that. The earth opened up and swallowed everyone I ever cared about; somehow I was the only one holding on, and when I climbed out with just a few bruises there was nothing left of them but the pictures I keep in the closet that I can't look at."

I can't think of anything to say.

"Let's go down the slide," I suggest.

"Okay."

"Let's go down together." It is my way of saying that I'm sorry for his family, and that I want to hug him but I don't know him, and that he is not the only one on that side of the quake's destruction.

"Okay."

He sits down first, legs apart, and I climb into the boat they make. He holds my arms tentatively and then lets go, so I grab his jeans on each side to make sure we stay together. Then he pushes off, and we sail into the dark static of the curled slide with only a few feet in front of us revealed at a time from the little bit of light coming through the plastic and the entrance we left. Then it is pitch black, and I hear the steady swish of us as we plummet to the earth through the chute of the slide. We finally slow down, and then the slide spits us out to a dazzling, sunny day.

Marissa

When she gets home Saturday night, Sam is asleep on the couch instead of back at his house where he belongs. "I didn't want to leave Joey here alone," he says when he wakes up to the sound of her getting a drink of water from the kitchen, but she can tell he does not want to go back to his lonely apartment.

"You can stay for awhile," she says with a shrug. "When I called earlier Joey sounded so happy I thought it was his birthday, so he must like you having around."

"We went to the park… he took me down the slide a few times."

"That's great."

She pulls out leftover baked ziti the boys made for dinner and sticks it in the microwave. As the cheese melts and then bubbles she can feel his eyes on her back, but she keeps hers on the rotating pasta dish. Sam is a good looking man, even with his chin stubble and shaggy hair, but she refuses to get into a relationship with another emotionally unstable man.

"He's a really special kid," Sam tells her as she grabs a fork and sits down at the table. "Really smart for his age."

"You're telling me. He practically reads minds."

"I hope not."

Sam stays at her house through the weekend. After they drop her son at school on Monday, their mutual day off, Marissa and Sam take their time walking back to the apartment. Their hands are just inches apart, accidentally brushing every few steps, but neither moves to take the other's hand. Instead they both talk about the bar they work at and comment on the traffic nearby: a red pick-up truck, a Mercedes, a Mini Cooper, a motorcycle.

"That's a 2012 Ducati 1199 Panigale," Marissa says without taking a second look.

Sam watches the bike pass them and then asks: "How the hell did you know that?"

"Back when I was a kid, every family in town had at least one motorcycle. It was rural Pennsylvania... there was nothing else to do but drive around looking at corn and race when tipping cows and stealing produce got boring. My grandpa had a Kawasaki Vulcan cruiser, both my uncles had Kawasaki Ninjas, and my dad had a red Ducati SuperSport. They used to talk for hours on the porch about Japanese versus Italian bikes, and I sat out there with them and listened until they sent me to bed. My dad was the fastest of all—they used to call him Quick Jim."

The roar of the motorcycle engine recedes like a fire engine siren, but they can still see the flash of yellow in the distance.

"If you're such a motorcycle expert, where's your bike?" Sam asks a little playfully, but she doesn't smile back. Her bike: a picture on her bedroom wall that her father gave her when she was ten years old, the edges of the magazine paper creased and frayed. The bike that he promised he was going to give her for her eighteenth birthday, since by then he would save up enough money from the shop to purchase a shiny new ride with a big purple bow on the front.

Sam talks, or at least his mouth does, but Marissa does not hear him. Instead she hears her father, his voice distant from up on the bike as he hands her the photo, and his low tones reverberate through her like the roar of an engine and get louder and louder as the memory comes back. It was the last time she ever heard his voice.

"You'll have to drive real carefully," her father told her with a pat on the head as he handed the photo to her from his seat. "You'll have to be aware. Eyes on the back of your head, mind awake and on the lookout for trouble, hands read to swerve at a moment's notice." Marissa nodded, eager to prove she was already on the path to maturity. Her older brother Jeremy sat twenty feet away on the grass, reading a boring book about something called 'philosophy' which he seemed to worship as much as her papa loved his bike, and if the motorcycle had sprouted wings and flown away he wouldn't have noticed. But Marissa loved the bike, loved the feel of the smooth gas tank under her hand, loved the way it purred like their cat Roger once the engine started.

Her father wore his favorite motorcycle jacket that day, a thick black jacket with silver detailing, and when he bent to hug her he crinkled under her jean jumper. Then he asked for his helmet, so she ran to the table in the corner of the garage to pick one of the three colorful globes to match his attire. After deciding on the silver one with black lightning bolts on the sides, her favorite by far because she wanted to be faster than lightening just like her dad, she ran back to his side and lifted the heavy helmet up like the communion blessing and her father put it on. His chin-length brown hair disappeared underneath the helmet and his face looked small through visor, and then he lifted it up so he could give her a goodbye kiss.

"Thanks, Riss," he said, patting her on the head

again. "Tell your mother not to wait up if I'm not back by nine." It meant he would miss dinner again, but she knew better than to argue. The road called him, and he always went; someday soon it would call her too.

She backed up three feet like he taught her, and then her father turned on the ignition, shifted into neutral, started the motorcycle, and then shifted again. Her hands clenched in the air as she gripped a fake clutch, miming his exact movements. The air from his motion past her blew through her hair, and then he was gone.

Immediately she was bored. She went over to Jeremy, who lay on his back with his book three inches from his face to block out the sunlight. He wore ripped jeans and an old band t-shirt of their father's, which on a nerdy fifteen year old was way too large to look cool.

"Hey Jer, want to play a game?" she asked, but he didn't look up. "How about a card game? Or hide and go seek?" Still no reaction, just the turning of pages.

Marissa went inside to find her mother, Peggy, who would at least talk to her. She was standing in the kitchen with her back to Marissa, the smell of some kind of lasagna wafting from the oven already. Her apron was covered in pasta sauce, and the remains of a spill had dripped down onto her jeans. There was flour on the counter, the remains of several slaughtered heads of broccoli on the cutting board, and a piece of carrot in her long red hair.

"Dad went biking," she told her mother, and then she climbed up to sit on the counter several feet from the splash zone. Her mother was an incredible cook—in just an hour there would be dish upon dish of delicious pasta, steamed corn, and probably an apple pie all set in the blue china that had been her grandmother's—but by the time she finished a meal, the entire kitchen would be covered in debris.

"Figures," Peggy said without looking up. "He always leaves right as I start on a huge meal. I should teach him a lesson and throw out the leftovers instead of putting them in the fridge for when he gets back." The spoon in her hand waved in emphasis, and tiny flecks of pasta sauce when flying in all directions.

The thought of her father returning home to find no food or drink after a long ride alarmed Marissa, but then she saw the tiny smile start in the corner of her mother's mouth and knew she would never actually do it. Instead she went back to work mixing and spilling her way around the kitchen, upturning the tea kettle and spilling half a container of salt on the floor in the process.

The buzzer on the counter began to ring, an incessant jingle like the lunch bell at school, and as Peggy bent down with two oven mitts over her hands Aunt Bernie ran through the screen door.

"Jesus, Bernie," Peggy exclaimed, jumping away from the oven, "you scared the skin off me." This expression was one of the many Peggy invented through the years, and whenever Marissa's father asked her where she picked up such nonsense, she told him it was just what people said. Of course the only person who said it was her, but the whole family found her sayings so amusing that they started using them too. Marissa giggled, but then she saw her aunt's panic-stricken face and stopped with a hiccup.

"What is it?" Peggy asked, and as soon as the words were out of her mouth Bernie's face wrinkled into a grimace and she began to cry.

Marissa had never seen a grownup cry before,

let alone her happy-go-lucky aunt who bought her the best Christmas presents and snuck her caramel candies from her purse when no one was looking. It was a moment she would remember all her life: the moment when she realized being older was no safer than being younger, that even when she grew up and moved away from her parents there would still be things that hurt her. There would still be monsters under the bed, though they would look and sound and smell different and she would have to bear their presence alone.

"It's Jim…" her aunt said, but the words were smeared in tears and the rest of her explanation was incomprehensible.

Her mother grabbed her aunt by the shoulders and shook her once, good and hard. "Tell me what's happened to him," Peggy said, but Bernie just looked at her and kept crying.

Finally she managed to get out the words motorcycle and accident, which made Peggy start shaking her again. "Is he okay?" she kept asking. "Where is he? Where's my husband?"

"Dead." Once the word was finally out of Bernie's mouth she sunk to the floor, and Peggy didn't move to help her. Instead she backed up to the counters on the far wall and leaned there, face blank, arms and hands shaking.

"No," Peggy said with such finality that Marissa felt it must not be true. "He can't be. Take me to him."

"You don't understand. There's no him left."

Before Marissa could recover from the shock, they heard the sound of smashed metal coming from outside. The pounding was louder than a bass drum but less harmonious—the way it sounds when two cars collide—and it kept getting louder until Marissa could not hear Bernie's cries. She imagined it was her father, crashing over and over again in a perpetual inferno.

"What the hell..." Peggy said, and she, Bernie and Marissa ran through the screen door to see what the commotion was about. The entire block's worth of small houses was owned by their family members, so if something was going on it was happening to one of them.

When they got outside Jeremy came running from the opposite direction. His face was splotched with red, and when he locked eyes with his sister she knew one someone had already told him. But instead of mentioning the accident he pointed down the street at their grandparents' house.

"It's Mimi," he said. "She's gone crazy."

All four of them ran through the high grass and down the road past four dirt driveways, past the fork in the road, past the sign for Cousin Lou's produce stand. As they got closer to Grandma Mimi's house the sound got louder and louder with every step, and though Marissa wanted to turn back because the noise scared her she was part of the wolf pack of her family and that was at least somewhat comforting. If she went back to the house she would be alone.

When they turned the corner, they saw a crowd of thirty people circled around Mimi's driveway. Marissa saw her grandpa first, in the center of the crowd on his knees with his head in his hands.

"My boy," he cried, gripping his hair and pulling so his upper torso pulled towards his knees. "My boy, my boy, my boy."

She looked for Mimi, but when she finally caught sight of she stopped cold and the other three instinctually stopped with her. In the middle of the circle Mimi stood in her favorite nightgown, the white one with small blue flowers along the neckline, which revealed the silhouette of her body just enough to make visitors uncomfortable. Her white hair stuck out in all directions, and her pale blue eyes were opened wide and focused on the work in front of her.

She held a baseball bat, one of Jim's from the look of it, and she raised it over her head and brought it down with a crack on the cruiser in front of her. It connected with the gear lever with a loud wham, and when she pulled away the lever was curved to the left. Before anyone could stop her she moved to the front, stalking the bike like prey, and then brought the bat down on the large headlight. As the glass rained down one of the neighbors moved to grab her, but by then she was hitting the small indicators and one flew directly towards the innocent bystander.

The whole circle backed up ten feet, and again she went at the gas tank and wheel spokes and gauges until every visible part on the bike was either dented or smashed. She panted like an animal, and her hands were white from her tight grip on the bat; a piece of metal or glass must have hit her cheek, since there was a smear of blood under her right eye.

Finally when Mimi decided the damage was done, she yelled in a high pitched voice that seeped with hatred: "I tried to stop you. I tried, but no, you had to teach every boy to ride so that they would spend their money on bikes instead of their families and would spend their time on the road instead of at home. Now look what it's done: my Jim is gone. Try riding another motorcycle, James, you just try. I'll do the same to your next bike, and the one after that, and I won't stop until I'm in heaven with my son."

Exhausted, Mimi threw the baseball bat near the knees of Marissa's grandpa and stormed back inside. The slam of the door made the crowd jump, and Marissa felt her mother tremble beside her.

"Marissa?" Sam asks as he puts his hand on her shoulder. She must have stopped talking when she got to the part about her grandmother, too distracted by the past to speak.

"Sorry, I'm fine. It just takes me back, that's all."

"Makes sense why you don't drive."

Sam pauses, then asks: "What happened after that?"

"Nothing for a while, just the funeral, once they brought back what was left of my father, and then the emptiness. My family barely spoke to each other for weeks until strange things started happening and they were forced to."

He leans in, and for the first time Marissa does not smell beer on his breath. "What kind of strange things?"

"It was the motorcycles on the block—they started breaking down one by one. Weeks would go by, and then one of my uncles would find his brake line cut or a dent in his gas tank or a light smashed. The last to go was my Uncle Brian's bike: they found it in a tree a month after my father's accident, pulled up and strung with rope... hoisted up on the back of someone's truck is my bet. No one was ever convicted, though three baseball bats washed up on the side of the river and a coil of rope was found in the school parking lot."

"Do you know who did it? Your grandfather? Your brother?"

"No... they wouldn't have gone toe to toe with my uncles, even if it was for their own good."

"Then who did all of it? Do you know?"

Marissa looks out to the road as another bike zooms by. She shakes her head, and then she smiles a little. "I didn't realize it then, but I figured it out when my son was born. The next week my boyfriend, Joey's father, parked his newly purchased motorcycle in front of the house. I loved him, but I couldn't even look at him after that without picturing my father."

Marissa takes Sam's hand. His palm is a little sweaty, but warm and comforting at the same time. "It was the women who smashed the bikes: the wives, mothers, grandmothers, and cousins of the bikers on the block. It was their retribution, and it worked; no man in my family ever rode again."

Sam's cell phone goes off on their way back to the house.

"Frankie," he says to Marissa, and when she nods he picks up.

"Hello?"

He listens for a few minutes, and she can tell something is wrong. He shakes his head like a swing as he listens, and though his hair falls into his eyes he doesn't blink.

"I understand," he says, then he hangs up.

"What did he say? Does he need one of us in?"

"He fired me."

"Oh. I'm so sorry." She feels selfish for thinking how glad she is that it isn't her losing her job.

"It's my fault. You can't just not call out for a few days and then expect forgiveness. Frankie needs servers at the bar when he needs them, and I wasn't there."

"What will you do?"

"What I was doing before, I guess."

"Which was...?"

"Absolutely nothing."

She thinks for a minute. "Well, until you get back on your feet, you could come stay with us."

What am I saying? she wonders, but the words are already out of her mouth. "I know a seven year old who would love to spend more time with you."

"Really? You'd let me hang out with your kid?"

"Of course. He needs someone around, and I could work more without worrying about him all the time."

They start walking back to the apartment, and she lets the air cool her hot skin. Neither of them says anything else, and then he takes her hand again; when they reach the apartment and start to climb the steps he doesn't let go. She can feel the hairs like moss on the back of his hand, and she runs her thumb back and forth over their softness before giving his hand a comforting squeeze.

Once inside Marissa pulls off her knee-high leather boots and Sam slips off his loafers, and then she removes both of their jackets and sweaters like she does with Joey when he comes in from the cold. She hangs them in the living room closet, the smell of wool and dust drifting out immediately, and wraps the scarves around their hangers and places their gloves into their coat pockets. Does she like this man, this stranger who appeared in her life so suddenly she had no time for a strong defense, or is it her motherly instinct that draws them together?

"Let's put on some music," he says to break the tension. He walks over to the CD player, a big black boom box from almost a decade ago that she bought for her dorm room, and before can say anything the quick piano of "Tiny Dancer" come through the speakers.

She lunges for the player, something between a tackle and a grande jeté, and in less than five seconds she finds the pause button and clicks. He stares at her, arm frozen in an outstretched position towards the boom box.

"Which one of us is the *Madman Across the Water* now?" Sam asks, trying to make a joke.

"I could make a strong argument for both sides."

She is aware of his eyes on her, waiting for her to say or do something to indicate it is going to be okay, like the minute after Joey breaks a glass. After hesitating, she presses play and begins to dance with him.

The End

Kelly Ann Jacobson lives in Falls Church, Virginia. Kelly is the author of the literary fiction novel *Cairo in White* and the young adult book *Dreamweaver Road*, as well as the editor of the book of essays *Answers I'll Accept*. She recently received her MA in Fiction at Johns Hopkins University, and she is the Poetry Editor for *Outside In Literary & Travel Magazine*. Her work, including her published poems, fiction, and nonfiction, can be found at www.kellyannjacobson.com.